Tom and Pippo See the Moon

PIPPO

HELEN OXENBURY

WALKER BOOKS
LONDON

One night when it was dark,
I saw the moon shining in the sky.

I asked Daddy all about the moon.
Daddy told me a man had been on
the moon and he had to get there
in a rocket.
I asked Daddy if
there was anybody
on the moon now,
and Daddy said no.

I asked Daddy
if Pippo and I
could go to
the moon, and Daddy said maybe,
but the moon is very far away.

If Pippo and I go to the moon
one day, I think Daddy should
come as well.

Anyway, tonight I think
we will just go to sleep.
Perhaps we will go to
the moon tomorrow.